The Christmas Bell

First published in Great Britain in 2003 by Brimax™,
A division of Autumn Publishing Limited
©2003 Autumn Publishing Limited
Appledram Barns, Chichester PO20 7EQ
Text and illustrations copyright © Autumn Publishing Limited 2003
© 1994 by Bohem press Zürich, Switzerland

McGraw Hill Children's Publishing

This edition published in the United States of America in 2003 by
Gingham Dog Press
an imprint of McGraw-Hill Children's Publishing,
a Division of The McGraw-Hill Companies
8787 Orion Place
Columbus, Ohio 43240-4027

www.MHkids.com

Library of Congress Cataloging-in-Publication Data is on file with the publisher.

Printed in China.

ISBN 1-57768-410-9

1 2 3 4 5 6 7 8 9 10 BRI 09 08 07 06 05 04 03

The Christmas Bell

By

Rolf Krenzer

Illustrated by

Maja Dusíková

GINGHAM DOG
PRESS

Columbus, Ohio

Long ago, a girl named Rachel lived with her father, who was a shepherd. Whenever her father stayed out late to tend his sheep, Rachel gazed up at the clear night sky and imagined her father looking up at the same sky as he led his sheep back home. But tonight, something was different. Tonight, the moon shone brighter. The stars glimmered more brilliantly than ever. The wind was but a gentle breeze. Tonight, it seemed as if the whole world was holding its breath.

Rachel felt certain that something important was about to happen. And it would happen soon.

The next day, Rachel found a shiny silver bell lying in the street with a red ribbon tied around its handle. She picked up the bell and smiled at the delicate chime it made. *Could this be what was important?* she wondered.

Rachel ran to Esther, a wise woman in the village.

"Esther," she called breathlessly, "I found a silver bell." Esther took the bell in her gnarled hands and jingled it.

"This is a special bell. So pure. So lovely. Where did you find it, child?"

Rachel explained.

"Then you must keep it close until the time is right. Then you can give it away."

"But how will I know when that is? Or who should receive it?"

"God has something important planned for you and will tell you when the time is right," said Esther.

Rachel nodded solemnly, proud to be part of God's plan. She was determined to be ready with the bell for whenever she would be needed.

While Rachel looked after the bell, a man named Joseph walked to Bethlehem with his wife, Mary, who was expecting a baby. They knocked on the doors of every inn in Bethlehem but could find no empty rooms. Finally, a kind innkeeper took pity on them.

"I have a stable that you may sleep in," he told them. "The straw is clean and the animals are gentle."

Joseph looked at Mary's tired face and knew the baby would be born soon. A stable would have to do. "You are very kind," he said.

The innkeeper led them to the stable and offered them a blanket so they would be warm.

That evening, Mary gave birth to a beautiful baby boy. She and Joseph wrapped him in the blanket and placed him in a manger.

"His name is Jesus," whispered Mary, "and he is the son of God."

Mary and Joseph hugged, thankful that their baby was safe and warm.

That same evening, in the hills surrounding Bethlehem, Rachel's father tended to his sheep with some other shepherds. Suddenly, a brilliant yellow light filled the sky. Within the light appeared angels from heaven. The shepherds fell to their knees, trembling with fear.

"Do not be afraid," said one of the angels. "We bring wonderful news! Tonight, God's Son was born in a stable. The baby's name is Jesus, and you will find him lying in a manger."

Then the angels gathered around the shepherds and sang, "Glory be to God in the highest. Peace on earth and goodwill to all men." The angels' sweet voices carried over the hills and into the night sky, filling the shepherds' hearts with joy.

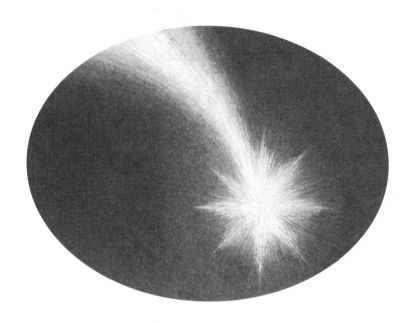

As the song ended, the angels told the shepherds to go to Bethlehem to find baby Jesus. "Follow the brightest star in the sky," they said. "It will lead you there."

At once, the shepherds packed up their belongings.

"We must bring gifts for the baby," said one of them.

Rachel's father looked around. *What could humble shepherds give to the Son of God?* he wondered. Then he knew. They would bring a sheep and her newborn lamb.

Rachel's father gathered the lamb into his arms. Then he and the shepherds set off for Bethlehem.

When they arrived, Rachel's father stopped at his home to speak with Rachel.

"My daughter," he said, "I have wonderful news." He told Rachel about the angels' visit. "You must come with us now to meet the baby."

Rachel couldn't believe her ears. Something important was happening! Now she knew just what to do with the bell. She ran to her room, grabbed the bell, and tied it around the lamb's neck. As the lamb shook its head, the bell jingled.

"You will give the lamb to the baby," said Rachel's father.

The shepherds set off once again to visit
Jesus, and Rachel carried the precious lamb
with the beautiful silver bell the entire way.
The closer they got, the more Rachel's heart
pounded in anticipation.

When they reached the stable, Rachel and
the shepherds entered quietly, so as not to
wake the baby.

Jesus lay in a manger just as the angels had said.

After a moment, Rachel's father beckoned to her. "It's time to give your present," he whispered.

As Rachel walked up to baby Jesus, her heart filled with wonder and joy.

Rachel peered over the manger to see the sleeping baby. She felt Mary gently put her arm around her.

"My name is Mary. Thank you for coming on this cold night."

As Rachel set the lamb down, the silver bell chimed softly.

"What a beautiful bell," said Mary, "but I can tell it is very special to you. The lamb is gift enough. You must keep the bell for yourself."

Rachel shook her head and explained how she had been saving the bell for something very important. "This is why I found the bell," she said, "so I could give it to baby Jesus. With all my heart, it's what I know I must do."

"I understand." Mary smiled and hugged Rachel. "Then we accept your gift. Thank you."

Rachel never forgot that cold winter's night. As she grew older, she told her children and grandchildren the story about finding the beautiful silver bell and giving it to baby Jesus. It was still the most important thing she'd ever done. And the love she had felt in the stable stayed with her for her entire life.

Now, at Christmas time, when the presents are all wrapped and placed under the tree, when the house is decorated with tinsel and lights, if you listen very, very carefully, you might be able to hear the faint sounds of a silver bell jingling today, just as it had for Rachel so long ago.

And as you hear that bell, imagine how it must have sounded on that cold night in Bethlehem long ago when Rachel gave her most precious gift to baby Jesus and felt his love all around her.